"HELLO READING books are a perfect introduction to reading. Brief sentences full of word repetition and full-color pictures stress visual clues to help a child take the first important steps toward reading. Mastering these storybooks will build children's reading confidence and give them the enthusiasm to stand on their own in the world of words."
—Bee Cullinan
Past President of the International Reading
Association, Professor in New York University's
Early Childhood and Elementary Education Program

"Readers aren't born, they're made. Desire is planted—planted by parents who work at it."
—Jim Trelease
author of *The Read-Aloud Handbook*

"When I was a classroom reading teacher, I recognized the importance of good stories in making children understand that reading is more than just recognizing words. I saw that children who have ready access to storybooks get excited about reading. They also make noticeably greater gains in reading comprehension. The development of the HELLO READING stories grows out of this experience."
—Harriet Ziefert
M.A.T., New York University School of Education
Author, Language Arts Module,
Scholastic Early Childhood Program

For Jon and Allison

VIKING
Published by the Penguin Group
Viking Penguin, a division of Penguin Books USA Inc.,
375 Hudson Street, New York, New York 10014, U.S.A.
Penguin Books Ltd, 27 Wrights Lane, London W8 5TZ, England
Penguin Books Australia Ltd, Ringwood, Victoria, Australia
Penguin Books Canada Ltd, 2801 John Street, Markham, Ontario, Canada L3R 1B4
Penguin Books (N.Z.) Ltd, 182-190 Wairau Road, Auckland 10, New Zealand

Penguin Books Ltd, Registered Offices: Harmondsworth, Middlesex, England

First published in 1991 by Viking Penguin, a division of Penguin Books USA Inc.

1 3 5 7 9 10 8 6 4 2

Text copyright © Harriet Ziefert, 1991
Illustrations copyright © Lillie James, 1991
All rights reserved
Library of Congress catalog card number: 90-50421
ISBN 0-670-84275-3

Printed in Singapore for Harriet Ziefert, Inc.

GOOD LUCK
BAD LUCK

Harriet Ziefert
Pictures by Lillie James

VIKING

It's good luck
to throw a shoe
over your shoulder.

It's bad luck
to break a shoelace.

One shoe off
and one shoe on—

that can also
bring bad luck.

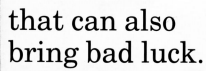

For good luck on the way
to school—

step on every crack
in the sidewalk...

or don't step on any!

It's bad luck if a black cat
crosses your path, unless—

you roll up your pants...

or cross your arms
and fingers and toes...

or take nine steps backward!

If the first robin you see
in spring flies up,

you will have good luck
for the rest of the year.

But if it flies down,
you won't.

Sprinkle salt on the tail
of a bird.

You may have good luck.

It's good luck when a spider
swings down in front of you.

And it's very, *very*, lucky
to find the first letter
of your name in a web.

But...

stepping on a spider
can bring bad luck.

Walking under a ladder can, too.

It's good luck to catch
a falling leaf.

It's also good luck
to find
a four-leaf clover.

Three and seven are
lucky numbers.

But thirteen can
mean bad luck.

It's lucky to see
the new moon
over your shoulder.

Make a wish and maybe
it will come true.

Wish on the first star
you see tonight:

Star light, star bright
The first star I see tonight
I wish I may, I wish I might
Get the wish I wish tonight.

Good luck!

BAKER & TAYLOR BOOKS